TIME-LIFE
Early Learning Program

The Three Storytellers of Or

TIME
LIFE for
Children
™

ALEXANDRIA, VIRGINIA

Note to Parents

In *The Three Storytellers of Or,* your child will take part in a learning adventure as a young boy named Jethro travels through a series of magical lands. Along the way, Jethro encounters a number of problems that the reader is invited to solve. Each challenge is designed to encourage your child's flexible-thinking skills by showing that not all problems have a single solution, and that there is often more than one way to arrive at a correct answer.

Jethro's journey begins in the "Land of Changes," where he solves riddles that involve sorting and classification. In "Topsy-Turvy Land," the goal is to spot what's wrong in each illustration. Jethro's next stop is a kingdom where opposites are shown in action. And in "Matching Mountain," he plays a game of wits with an irascible man of stone.

Finally, Jethro meets three story-tellers, flexible thinkers who each invent a different tale about the same picture. Jethro and your child return home with many new stories of their own—as well as greatly expanded imaginations.

A Gift from Uncle Toussaint

It was Jethro's seventh birthday, and his party had been a whirlwind of fun and surprises. Tired but happy, he sat on his bed playing with his presents. Suddenly his favorite uncle appeared in the doorway.

"Here's one more little gift!" boomed Uncle Toussaint. He handed Jethro a box that rattled.

Jethro unwrapped the present and dumped it out on his bed.

"It's a magic puzzle!" Uncle Toussaint explained. "Put all the pieces together, and the puzzle will tell you a story! I'll come back tomorrow to see how you're doing."

Before Jethro could ask how a puzzle can tell a story, Uncle Toussaint was gone.

Jethro pushed his other presents aside and eagerly began putting the puzzle together. He worked late into the night, and slowly the puzzle took shape.

In it were all sorts of strange sights: a zebra standing on two legs, a fish walking on its fins and carrying an umbrella, a huge pile of boulders, and a flower garden filled with curious blossoms.

Just as Jethro
was about to finish the
puzzle, he made a terrible
discovery: One piece was missing!
The missing piece belonged in the middle
of the puzzle. Next to it was a door, with half a key
stuck in the lock. "The other half of that key must be on
the missing piece," thought Jethro. Then he wondered if some-
one might be holding the key—and turning it in the lock!

"How will I ever learn the story of the puzzle without that missing piece?" Jethro searched and searched, but he could not find the piece. Finally, he fell exhausted onto his bed.

"What could the story be?" Jethro mumbled. "What could it be? What could it be? What could it be?"

Jethro blinked his eyes. Standing before him was the zebra from his puzzle!

"Where am I?" Jethro wondered out loud. To his astonishment, the zebra flicked her tail and answered him:

You are where you should not be—
Everything here is the same as me!

"How can you say that everything's the same as you?" Jethro demanded. "You're the only zebra around!"

The zebra tossed her mane and laughed:

Skunks smell funny, penguins are birds;
A chessboard is part of a game.
Yet they all have something in common with me—
Something that makes us the same!

Then she asked, "Don't you see what it is?"

Jethro gazed at the scene for a few moments before answering the zebra's question.

How do you think the skunk, the penguin, and the chessboard are the same as the zebra?

"Black and white!" cried Jethro. "The things here are black and white—*that's* why they're the same as you! By the way, my name's Jethro."

"Mine is Camille," said the zebra. "And this is my kingdom, the Land of Changes."

"Perhaps you can help me," said Jethro. "I'm trying to learn the story of this puzzle. See? You're in it!"

"How wonderful!" said Camille. "The story must be all about me! But there's only one way to find out: Let's show that puzzle to the Three Storytellers of Or!"

Before Jethro could ask about the storytellers, he noticed that everything had changed.

"Hey, those things aren't black and white!" he exclaimed. "Nothing looks the same as you anymore!"

Camille gave a snort and replied:

> *A tiger can be like a beach ball;*
> *Are you getting the hang of this game?*
> *A zebra can be like a barber pole—*
> *Now tell me how they're the same!*

Jethro furrowed his brow and studied everything around him. Then a smile lit up his face.

How would you answer Camille's riddle?

"Stripes!" yelled Jethro. "You all have stripes! Everything *has* changed—but it's still the same as you!"

"Right you are!" Camille nodded.

"Now, about those storytellers you mentioned—" began Jethro.

"You've never heard of the Storytellers of Or?" cried Camille. "Why, they know more stories than anyone! They're sure to know the story of that puzzle!"

"Super!" said the excited Jethro. "Where are they?"

"The Land of Or lies far away," replied Camille. "We must journey through many lands to get there."

Meanwhile, everything had changed again. "There's no way you fit in now!" Jethro challenged Camille.

"Oh, but I assure you that I do!" the zebra retorted.

The chair, the table, the grill, and I
Have something in common—it's true!
We all stand up on the very same things—
But I see that you only have two!

Jethro looked up and around, but he was stumped. Then he looked down, and the answer came to him.

In what way are these things like Camille?

"Four legs!" Jethro shouted. "Everything here has four legs!"

"Bravo!" cheered Camille. "You've made short work of three riddles in a row!"

"Great!" said Jethro. "But to tell you the truth, I'd really like to solve the mystery of this puzzle."

"You'll soon have a chance," said Camille. "Look—we've almost reached the border of my kingdom!"

Once again, Jethro's surroundings had undergone a complete transformation. And once again, Camille burst into verse:

What helps a monkey swing through the trees?
What keeps a kangaroo from falling to her knees?
What does a whale use to speed through the sea?
Here's a little hint for you: There's even one on me!

"That's a toughie!" said Jethro. He bit his lower lip and surveyed the scene. Then he cried out, "Aha!"

Everything here has something in common with Camille—can you see what it is?

"Tails!" hollered Jethro. "You all have tails! Wow—everything in the Land of Changes really *is* the same as you!"

"That's right!" said Camille. "The same in different ways!"

Jethro tugged on the zebra's tail. "Come on, we have to find the Storytellers of Or!"

"Uh-oh!" cried Camille. "I just remembered that I can't go with you!"

For I must always be
Where things are just like me!

"Don't be silly," said Jethro. "You *will* be with something like you— you'll be with me! Don't you see? We *both* want to learn the story of the puzzle!"

That was all Camille needed to hear. She told Jethro to hop on her back, and the two of them set out together for Topsy-Turvy Land.

A Topsy-Turvy Journey

Jethro and Camille entered Topsy-Turvy Land and found themselves surrounded by strange sights.

"Excuse me," said Jethro to a fish holding an umbrella, "could you direct us to the Land of Or?"

"No time for that!" the fish replied without stopping. "I'm on my way to a race!"

"But you're a fish!" said Camille. "Why do you need that umbrella?"
"In case it rains, silly!" the fish explained as he hurried by. "You
wouldn't want me to get wet, would you?"
Then the fish disappeared down the road.

Camille and Jethro caught up with the fish carefully crossing a pond on stilts.

"Things sure are odd around here!" said Jethro. "I just saw a frog with wings, a bird wearing shoes, and hot dogs growing on a tree!"

"What's so odd about that?" asked the fish. "This is Topsy-Turvy Land! What looks wrong to you looks right to us! By the way, my name's Bow-tie."

HOW MANY TOPSY-TURVY THINGS CAN YOU FIND HERE?

"I'm Jethro," the boy replied. "This is Camille, and—hey! You're the fish in my puzzle!" Jethro showed his jigsaw puzzle to the fish.

"Whoa!" said Bow-tie. "I *am* in your puzzle! What a thrill!" Then, glancing at a distant clock tower, he exclaimed, "Whoops! Gotta go! I'm late for a race!" And he hurried off.

"Let's follow that fish!" yelled Camille. "He may know the story of the puzzle!"

"Watch out for that pig in pajamas!" Jethro shouted. "Steer clear of that tiger in tennis shoes! And don't run into that—"

TODAY'S SPECIAL

Find more than 8 things that are not quite right!

CRASH!!!

"We'll never catch him now!" moaned Jethro.

"Forget the fish!" cried Camille.
"Just get me out of these scrambled eggs!"

When Jethro and Camille finally caught up with Bow-tie, he was about to enter a most ridiculous race.

"You can't get around on wheels that are square!" cried Jethro.

"You're right!" said Bow-tie with a big smile. "But as everyone knows, topsy-turvy races don't go anywhere!"

"Can you tell us why you're in Jethro's puzzle?" Camille interrupted.
"I wish I could!" Bow-tie sadly responded. "But it's a mystery to me!"
"Then why not come with us?" asked Jethro. "We're going to ask some storytellers all about my puzzle!"
"That's a splendid idea!" said Bow-tie. So the three new friends went in search of the Storytellers of Or.

TOPSY-TURVY LAND

KINGDOM OF OPPOSITES

FINISH

LOOK SHARP! SPOT AS MANY ODDITIES AS YOU CAN.

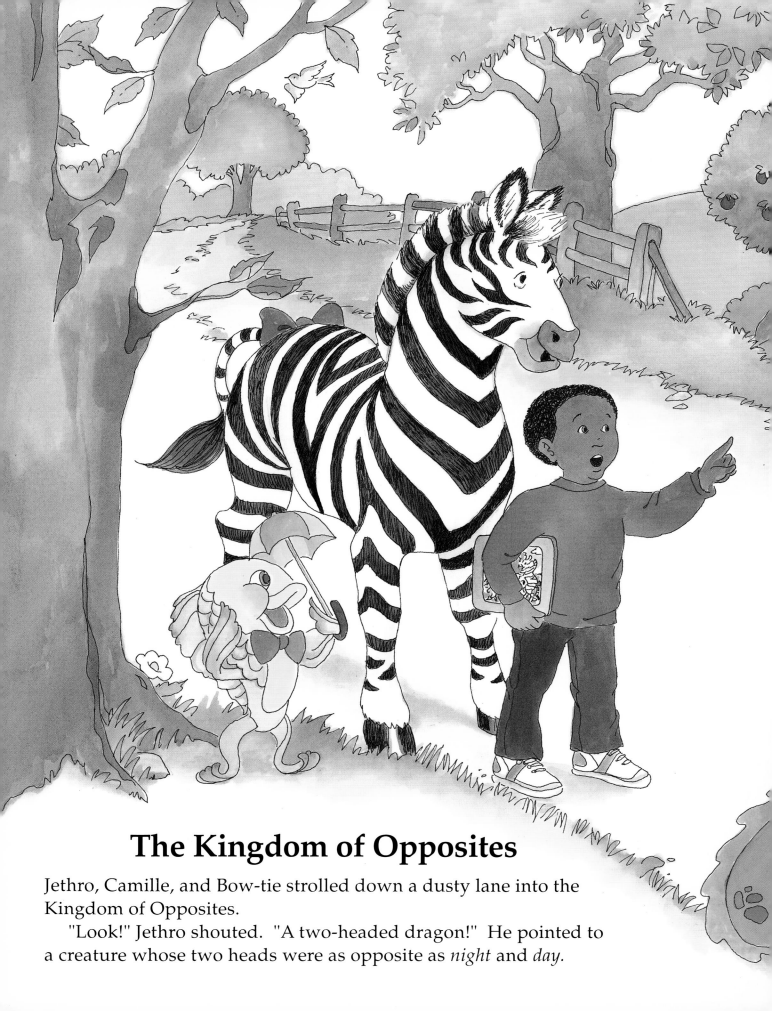

The Kingdom of Opposites

Jethro, Camille, and Bow-tie strolled down a dusty lane into the Kingdom of Opposites.

"Look!" Jethro shouted. "A two-headed dragon!" He pointed to a creature whose two heads were as opposite as *night* and *day*.

"You've *never* met a two-headed dragon?" asked one of the dragon's surprised heads.

"I've never met a *one*-headed dragon!" said Jethro.

"Don't you know that two heads are better than one?" laughed the dragon's other head.

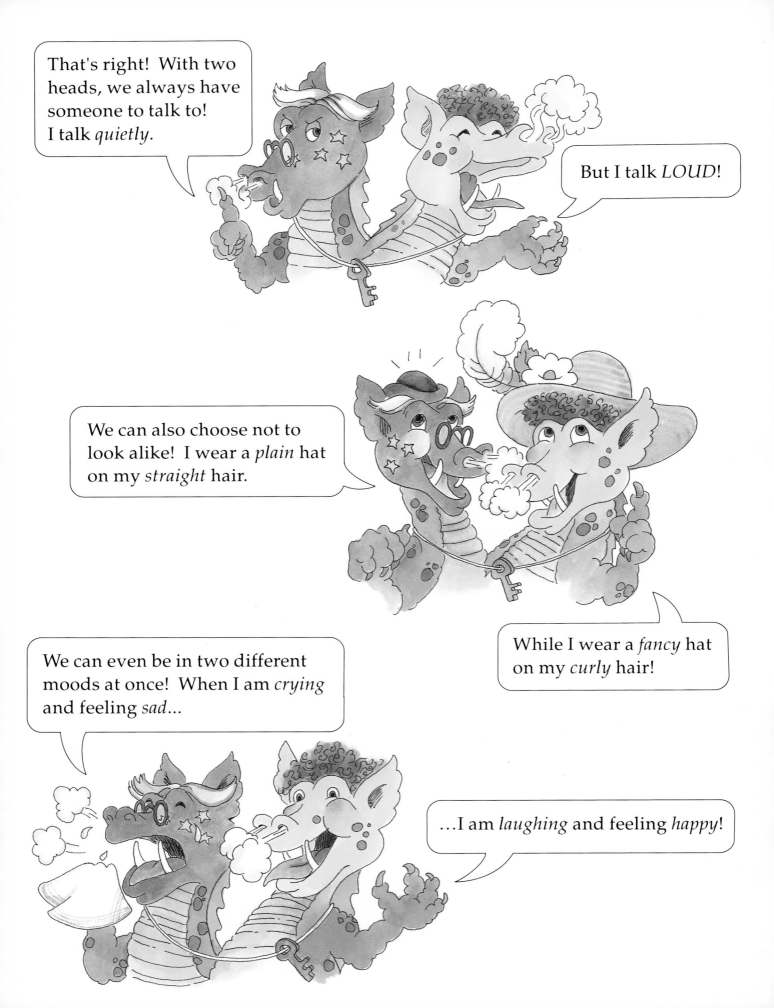

"Wow!" said Jethro. "Two heads really *are* better than one. If you put your heads together, I'll bet you can help us find the Three Storytellers of Or."

"We can't take you all the way to Or," said the dragon. "But we will guide you through the Kingdom of Opposites. It's a rough journey, though. Many turn back."

They set out at once, trudging slowly across a *bright, dry, dusty* desert.

"I can't bear this heat," moaned Camille. "Maybe we should turn back."

"Don't give up now," said Jethro. "Look! We're almost to the edge of the desert."

All of a sudden they were sloshing through a *dark, wet, muddy* rain forest.

"I hate getting wet!" Bow-tie complained. "What if my umbrella springs a leak? I wish I'd stayed home."

"Your umbrella's fine," said Jethro. "Besides, this rain can't last forever."

Sure enough, the rain quickly ended, and they found themselves climbing *up* a *jagged* mountain.

"I'm no mountain goat," puffed Camille. "I've had it with this climbing! I'm going home!"

No sooner had she spoken than they went sliding *down* the *smooth* side of the mountain into a beautiful valley.

"I told you this trip would be full of *ups* and *downs*," said the dragon.

Next they reached a rope bridge that stretched across a bottomless canyon. They walked *over* the bridge and *under* a massive stone arch.

Finally, they came to a wide river.

"This is the end of the Kingdom of Opposites," said the dragon. He pointed to the other side of the river. "To reach Or, you have only to cross this river and climb Matching Mountain."

The signs read:

KINGDOM OF OPPOSITES

MATCHING MOUNTAIN

"Here is a key," added the dragon, "to remember us by."

Jethro put the key in his pocket and thanked the dragon for guiding them through the Kingdom of Opposites. Then Camille waded into the water and started to swim across.

"Wait!" shrieked Bow-tie. "I can't cross that river! I might get wet!"

Suddenly the *calm* day turned *stormy*. Before Bow-tie knew what was happening, a gust of wind caught his umbrella and lifted it high into the air. Clinging tightly to the handle, he sailed across the river and landed on the other side—completely dry.

"What's taking you so long?" Bow-tie called to Camille and Jethro, who were still crossing the river. "Let's hurry up and get to Or."

Together again, the trio of travelers headed happily toward Matching Mountain.

Matching Mountain

Jethro and his friends came to a steep hill covered with gnarled trees. As they climbed upward, the day grew even darker. The birds stopped singing and the wind began to howl.

"Halt!" roared a voice like thunder. "Who dares to enter the kingdom of Boulder Man?"

"We're on our way to see the Storytellers of Or," explained Jethro, though he could not see who was talking. "Who–or what–are you?"

The mountain quivered and quaked. Then it rose straight up out of the ground.

"I am Boulder Man!" bellowed the mountain. "Beat me at my game of wits and I shall let you pass!"

Boulder Man reached into his pocket, which was shaped like a cave, and held out a pair of boots. "What goes with these?"

"A foot!" answered Jethro.
"An umbrella!" suggested Bow-tie.
"A muffler!" cried Camille.
"Wrong, wrong, and wrong again!" yelled Boulder Man.
"Rain goes with boots, because whenever it rains, you put on
your boots! You've lost the game, so turn around and go home!"

"Now wait just a minute!" shouted Jethro. "A foot goes with boots because you wear your boots on your feet."

"And an umbrella goes with boots," said Bow-tie, "because they both keep you dry."

"And a muffler goes with boots," continued Camille, "because they both keep you warm."

Boulder Man stamped his foot in frustration, making the earth tremble beneath them. Then he pulled a book from another pocket and asked, "What goes with this?"

"A school!" offered Jethro.

"Eyeglasses!" said Bow-tie.

"A bed!" ventured Camille.

"Incorrect, not right, and doubly wrong again!" cried Boulder Man. "The answer is a library—*that's* where a book belongs!"

"But not every question has a single answer," Jethro protested. "All four answers are right! A book goes with a school, for instance, because we read all kinds of wonderful stories in class!"

"And a book goes with glasses," explained Bow-tie, "because I can't read one unless I'm wearing my reading glasses."

"And a book goes with a bed," declared Camille, "because I read myself to sleep every night."

"Arrrgh!" fumed Boulder Man. "I just *hate* it when I don't win every game I play!" He reached into yet a third pocket, pulled out a hammer, and asked them, "All right, what's the one thing that goes with this?!"

"A toolbox!" cried Jethro.

"A nail!" guessed Bow-tie.

"A house!" said Camille.

"Nope, no, and nuh-uh!" hollered Boulder Man. "The answer is a thumb! Whenever I take this hammer from my toolbox to put a nail in the birdhouse I'm building, I miss and hit my thumb! Now I've won the game, so good-bye!"

"But you yourself just solved the riddle in several different ways!" Jethro pointed out. "Toolbox is right, because that's where you *keep* the hammer.

"Nail is right, because that's what you *hit* with the hammer.

"And house is right, too, because that's what you *build* with the hammer!"

Boulder Man threw up his craggy arms in defeat.

"I hate to admit it," he said in a gravelly voice, "but you've beaten me at my own game of wits!" Then he pointed to a sign in the distance and said, "That way lies the Land of Or."

"Hey, you're in my puzzle!" Jethro suddenly exclaimed. "Why don't you come with us?"

"A majestic idea!" cried Boulder Man. "Hop aboard!"

So Jethro and his friends clambered up onto the mountain's wide shoulders, and the four of them set off to discover the story of the puzzle.

LAND
OF OR

MATCHING
MOUNTAIN

The Three Storytellers of Or

Boulder Man, with his fellow travelers bouncing on his shoulders, journeyed miles with every step. Soon they came to a flower patch beside an old vine-covered door. It was the door from Jethro's puzzle! As they approached, three huge blossoms rose up from the garden.

"Welcome!" one of the flowers called out gaily. "We are the Three Storytellers of Or." The flowers bowed on their slender stems.

"Oh, please, great storytellers," said Jethro. "Can you tell us the story of this puzzle?"

Jethro held out the puzzle for the storytellers to see.
"That puzzle has a marvelous story!" cried the first flower.
"Allow me to tell it to you!"

nce upon a time, a clever and magical zebra named Camille was hiking through a forest when she met a massive stone man next to a door. Waterfalls of tears streamed down his rocky sides, drenching a little fish at his feet.

"Whatever is the matter?" Camille asked sweetly.

"Oh, woe is me!" the stone man answered. "I've lost the key to that door, and my birthday presents are on the other side!"

"Maybe I can help," Camille said. She rose up on her hind legs, pointed to the door, and cried out, "ARBEZ!" (That's "ZEBRA" spelled backward.) A great puff of smoke poured out of the keyhole. When the smoke cleared, the key was in the lock!

"However can I thank you?" cried the stone man as he rushed to open the door.

"No thanks are necessary," answered Camille. "I do this sort of thing all the time." Then she waved farewell and trotted merrily on her way.

"That was a wonderful story," sighed Camille.

"Well, *I* thought it was ridiculous!" said Boulder Man. "Who ever heard of a stone man crying?"

"But that's not the only story of the puzzle!" said the second flower. "It could be an entirely different tale!"

nce upon a time, there was a big-hearted stone mountain named Boulder Man. One day, as he sat by a flower garden, the door next to him burst open. Out jumped a fish and a zebra.

"Help!" the fish shrieked. "It's the Terrible Tickle Fiend! I can't take any more. I've laughed so much my sides hurt."

Just then a strange creature with a huge grin and 10 arms rushed through the door.

"Hee, hee, hee!" the Tickle Fiend giggled, reaching for the zebra. "I'll make you laugh until your stripes fall off!"

"Hold it right there!" Boulder Man boomed. "I won't have you tickling my friends!"

The sniggering fiend halted in alarm. Boulder Man picked him up and pushed him back through the door.

"Now," said Boulder Man, "I have just the thing to make sure he doesn't come back." He reached into a cavernous pocket and pulled out a hammer, followed by a boot, a box of bandages, a book, a library card, and finally an old gold key.

"I knew I'd find a use for this some day," he cried as he carefully locked the door.

"Boulder Man, you're our hero!" cheered the fish and the zebra.

"Now *that* was a great story!" said Boulder Man.

"Well," said the last storyteller, "that could be the story. *Or* it could be a fish tale!"

nce upon a time, there was a land where everyone hurried. They never listened to music or stopped to smell the flowers that grew beside the road. And no one *ever* smiled.

In the middle of this somber land was an ancient door that stood next to a mountain and a field of flowers. The key to the door was lost, and everyone had long since forgotten what was on the other side. But one day, a wise fish named Bow-tie began searching for the key.

"What are you doing?" asked a passing zebra.

"I want to see what's on the other side of that door," said the fish.

Suddenly Bow-tie spotted an old gold key shining in the ivy. He put the key in the lock and turned it. Immediately, music erupted from the door. The zebra reared up on her hind legs and clapped. The mountain broke into a craggy grin. All over the land, everyone paused, listened—and *smiled*. In fact, they exploded into peals of laughter; they tittered, they guffawed, they roared. Never had they had such fun.

From then on, everyone slowed down. They stopped to admire beautiful sunsets. They talked for hours about nothing at all. They whistled and they hummed, they smiled and they laughed—and it was all because of Bow-tie!

"I liked that story best of all," said Bow-tie. "I can't believe you told us three different stories about just one puzzle!"

"That's right," said Camille. "You've told a story about each of us…but none about Jethro!"

"We're sorry," the storytellers answered. "We tell only one story each. Besides, Jethro is not in the puzzle."

"That's okay," said Jethro. "There *is* another story, and I know what it is!" Then he reached into his pocket, pulled out the dragon's key, and put it in the lock.

"It's the puzzle!" Bow-tie exclaimed.
"And Jethro was on the missing piece!" cried Camille,
jumping up and pointing at Jethro.

"I had the answer to the puzzle all the time!" laughed Jethro. "But I didn't realize it!"

Then he turned the key in the lock and walked through the door.

Jethro opened his eyes to the sound of a
splash. It was morning, and he was back in his bed.
"It must have been a dream!" thought Jethro. Then he
looked at his fishbowl. It had been empty the night before, but
now there was a fish swimming in it—a fish with a bow tie on its
neck! Jethro smiled to himself: Perhaps it hadn't been a dream after all!

Just then, Uncle Toussaint walked through the open door.
"Good morning!" he said. "Did you discover the story of the puzzle?"
"*The* story?" laughed Jethro. "Uncle Toussaint, I could tell you a lot more than one story about that puzzle!"
And that's exactly what Jethro did.

TIME-LIFE for CHILDREN™
Publisher: Robert H. Smith
Managing Editor: Neil Kagan
Editorial Directors: Jean Burke Crawford,
    Patricia Daniels, Allan Fallow, Karin Kinney, Sara Mark
Editorial Coordinator: Elizabeth Ward
Director of Marketing: Margaret Mooney
Product Manager: Cassandra Ford
Assistant Product Manager: Shelley L. Schimkus
Business Manager: Lisa Peterson
Assistant Business Manager: Patricia Vanderslice
Production Manager: Prudence G. Harris
Administrative Assistant: Rebecca C. Christoffersen
Special Contributor: Jacqueline A. Ball

Produced by Joshua Morris Publishing, Inc.
Wilton, Connecticut 06897.
Series Director: Michael J. Morris
Creative Director: William N. Derraugh
Editor: Lynn Offerman
Illustrator: Linda Weller
Author: Marc Spiegel
Designer: Nora Voutas
Design Consultant: Francis Morgan

CONSULTANTS
Dr. Lewis P. Lipsitt, an internationally recognized specialist on childhood development, was the 1990 recipient of the Nicholas Hobbs Award for science in the service of children. He serves as science director for the American Psychological Association and is a professor of psychology and medical science at Brown University, where he is director of the Child Study Center.
Dr. Judith A. Schickedanz, an authority on the education of preschool children, is an associate professor of early childhood education at the Boston University School of Education, where she also directs the Early Childhood Learning Laboratory. Her published work includes *More Than the ABC's: Early Stages of Reading and Writing Development* as well as several textbooks and many scholarly papers.

First printing. Printed in Hong Kong.
Published simultaneously in Canada.

Time Life Inc. is a wholly owned subsidiary of THE TIME INC. BOOK COMPANY.

TIME-LIFE is a trademark of Time Warner Inc. U.S.A.

Time Life Inc. offers a wide range of fine publications, including home video products. For subscription information, call 1-800-621-7026, or write TIME-LIFE BOOKS, P.O. Box C-32068, Richmond, Virginia 23261-2068.

Library of Congress Cataloging-in-Publication Data
The Three storytellers of Or.

    p. cm.–(Time-Life early learning program)
    Summary: Seven-year-old Jethro finds the solution to a puzzle with a missing piece with the help of three storytellers from the Land of Or.

    ISBN 0-8094-9283-0 (trade).—ISBN 0-8094-9284-9 (lib. bdg.)

    [1. Puzzles—Fiction. 2. Problem solving—Fiction.] I. Time-Life for Children (Firm) II. Series.
PZ7.T415 1991
[E]—dc20   91-24056
                                                                  CIP
                                                                  AC